So You've Adopted A Sibling

Written by Holly Marlow

Illustrated by Zoe Marlow

DEDICATION

For my amazing children, who inspired me to create this book. I love you both incredibly much, and I always will.

ACKNOWLEDGEMENTS

Endless thanks to my wonderful husband Jon, who has supported me in so many ways. Love you always.

Special thanks to my imaginative superstar, Zoe, for creating the beautiful artwork that makes this book fun!

So you've adopted a baby brother or sister, huh? Whoop whoop! Welcome to the club! My family adopted my baby brother last year.

I know it can be pretty strange when things start to change, but you're in luck! I have some top tips for you!

So my first top tip is: eat your favourite food first! I used to save chips 'til last, but my brother eats his super-fast, then screams for mine if he sees them on my plate! I eat my chips first now!

Sometimes when you adopt a baby, they are used to different meals, so you have to try some new foods, so they can still have their favourite meals.

I was annoyed at first, and my brother didn't like some of my favourite foods either, but actually we have both found some new foods that we like!

My next tip is: make sure you are in charge of putting the cutlery on the table, so you can make sure you both get the RIGHT cutlery. I call myself the Cutlery Monitor.

Babies want to be just like their big brother or sister. My little brother always asks for the purple cup, because he knows I like that one.

Sometimes we do this thing called a "compromise" where everyone gets a BIT of what they want, so I have the purple cup with the yellow lid and he has the yellow cup with the purple lid.

I'm pretty good at taking turns, but my little brother is still learning. Sometimes he forgets that it's not kind to snatch. I try to stay calm and explain that I am still using that toy.

Sometimes I ask my parents to help, but usually I just wait. My little brother gets bored quickly, so he only plays with toys for a few minutes, then I can take it back when he gets distracted.

Some of my toys aren't safe for my brother. I'm sensible and wouldn't put small things in my mouth, but my little brother might. We keep the toys with small parts in cupboards he can't open.

I can't play with those toys when my brother is around, because he gets upset that he can't join in. I don't mind really, because I want my fragile toys to be kept safe, so that he won't damage them!

My little brother likes to watch baby TV shows. They are mostly fun, but sometimes boring. My parents tell me when it's my turn to watch what I want to.

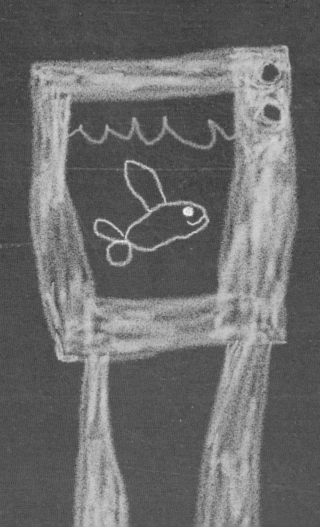

If my brother is watching something boring, I just play with toys instead. It's a good time to play with the things he's too little to play with!

Babies can be NOISY. My baby brother is always singing or chatting!

And when he cries, it's REALLY loud! So be prepared to cover your ears, or maybe you could even wear ear plugs!

When my brother first moved in, he was a bit nervous about going in the bath. He didn't know we would keep him safe, so he just watched me playing in the bath at first.

He could see that our parents kept me safe, then he felt brave enough to come in.

Now he loves baths! He gets so excited, the water goes EVERYWHERE! I tell him he's a cheeky little fish and he laughs and laughs!

I recommend some goggles for bath time, if your little brother or sister is as splashy as mine!

When my little brother naps, I have to be SUPER quiet, so he can sleep. I like nap times, because we can play games that he can't, like cards.

It is a bit frustrating if he wakes up while we are in the middle of a game. Mum says he can't wait. He doesn't understand that she will come and get him in a minute, so she has to go straight away.

Bedtime is a bit different now. I used to pick a story for one of my parents to read me before bed, but now my little brother and I each choose a story. Sometimes I help him pick his!

After a few months, my parents were able to fill out some paperwork that sounded very boring, but meant that my brother would have the same surname as us, so we had a cake to celebrate that we match!

Well, that's all my top tips for being the big sibling! Sometimes it's difficult to get used to things changing, but it's worth it to have a fun little brother or sister to play with!

the end

Sharing this story with your child

It can be overwhelming for children when a new brother or sister joins the family. When this happens through adoption, this often includes a lot of changes to routine in order to accommodate the routine that the adopted child is used to.

So You've Adopted a Sibling has been created to help support and stimulate discussion around some of the emotions that elder siblings may experience about their younger sibling joining the family. If discussion does not arise naturally as you progress through the story, try asking your child some of these questions. If they express frustration, you can empathise and agree that sometimes change is hard and frustrating.

1. What do you think is different about our mealtimes now? Have you enjoyed trying some new meals? Do you and your sibling have the same favourite foods, or different?
2. Can you think of any compromises we've had to make, like the children who swapped cup lids in this story so that they could both have a bit of the purple cup?
3. Are you and your brother or sister used to taking turns yet? Is it harder with some toys than others?
4. Have we had to put some toys away out of reach of your little sibling, to keep them safe? When do we find time to play with those? Is that a bit annoying, or do you not mind, because we have so many other fun toys that are safe for your sibling?
5. Do you and your sibling like the same TV shows? Which ones are your favourites? What do you like to do while your sibling's favourite TV shows are on?
6. Is your brother or sister noisy? Which of you is noisier?
7. How are bath times different for us now? Do you and your sibling have baths together? Is it fun? Was your sibling nervous about going in the bath, like the brother in the story?
8. Does your sibling have naps? What do we do during naptime?
9. How is your bedtime routine different now? Do you think it will change again, as you and your brother or sister get older?
10. What top tips would **you** have for someone else who has adopted a little brother or sister?

Also by Holly Marlow

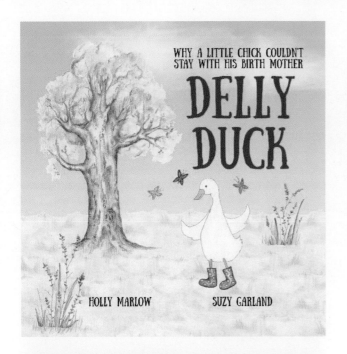

WHY A LITTLE CHICK COULDN'T
STAY WITH HIS BIRTH MOTHER

DELLY DUCK

HOLLY MARLOW   SUZY GARLAND

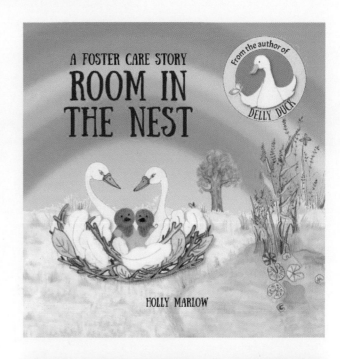

A FOSTER CARE STORY
ROOM IN THE NEST

From the author of DELLY DUCK

HOLLY MARLOW

Cousins by Adoption

Written by Holly Marlow
Illustrated by Zoe Marlow

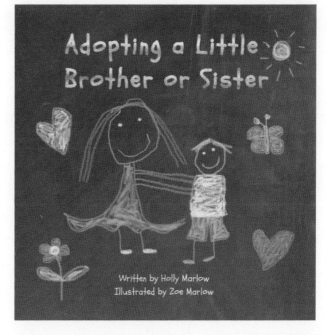

Adopting a Little Brother or Sister

Written by Holly Marlow
Illustrated by Zoe Marlow

About The Author

Holly Marlow is a British author and parent to both biological and adopted children. Holly strives for a gentle/therapeutic parenting style and this has led her to create stories to help children to understand some of the emotional and practical complexities of foster care and adoption.

Holly enjoys travelling (especially searching for chameleons, geckos and snakes in the wild parts of Africa) and learning foreign languages. Holly has fibromyalgia and has spent a lot of time trying to raise awareness of the chronic pain condition, giving presentations in schools and universities. Holly also enjoys baking and gardening, and is terrible at both.

This story is illustrated by Holly's talented daughter, Zoe, who at age 5 enjoys soft play, parks and creating her own illustrated stories and plays. Zoe was eager to provide the illustrations for this book. She created them in less than 10 minutes and has been wondering for months why it took her mother so long to finish the book.

Printed in Great Britain
by Amazon

85327043R00016